Six of Cups

A SHORT, FIRST LOVE, MAGICAL REALISM, SECOND CHANCE ROMANCE

TAROT FANTASIES
BOOK FOUR

JAX WILDER

Six of Cups

Tarot Fantasies Series
Jax Wilder

RAINBOW QUARTZ PUBLISHING

SIX OF CUPS© 2024 BY JAX WILDER

PUBLISHED BY RAINBOW QUARTZ PUBLISHING

EDMONDS WA, 98026

ISBN: 978-1-961714-49-6 FIRST EDITION: 2024

COVER DESIGN BY MIRANDA TOWNSEND

INTERIOR DESIGN BY MIRANDA TOWNSEND

TAROT CARD DESCRIPTION BY LORELAI HAMILTON FROM THE BOOK TEENAGE TAROT – USED WITH PERMISSION.

FOR PERMISSIONS OR INQUIRIES, PLEASE CONTACT:

RAINBOW QUARTZ PUBLISHING

RAINBOWQUARTZPUBLISHING@GMAIL.COM

WWW.RQPUBLISHING.COM

To first loves—

For the butterflies, the late-night talks, and the memories that never fade.

You taught us the beauty of vulnerability, the thrill of connection, and the bittersweet taste of what it means to truly care.

Thank you for showing us that love, in all its forms, is a journey worth taking.

Jax Wilder

6 of Cups

"I AM THE VESSEL OF FOND RECOLLECTIONS
AND HEARTFELT CONNECTIONS TO THE PAST," 6
OF CUPS.

Key Words and Phrases:
Nostalgia and childhood memories
Innocence and simplicity
Reconnecting with the past
Fondness for old friendships and relationships
Sentimentality and emotional warmth
Sharing kindness and generosity
Receiving gifts or unexpected surprises
Inner child and playful innocence
Embracing joy and wonder

The Six of Cups card is all about nostalgia and memories from childhood. Remember those simpler times when life felt carefree and full of wonder? It's like taking a trip down memory lane and reminiscing about the good old days.

The Six of Cups goes beyond mere reflection; it emphasizes the importance of bringing the comforting emotions of warmth and nostalgia into the present. Don't forget to cherish the memories and relationships that shaped who you are today.

—LORELAI HAMILTON, AUTHOR OF *TEENAGE TAROT*
AND *TAROT TALES & MAGIC SPELLS*

One

I went to the Arcane Room to forget, but the Arcane Room had other plans for me. Living with the memories was hard enough, but being reminded of my biggest mistake—that was too much.

When I stepped through the heavy wooden doors of the Arcane Room, the air shifted around me, thick with the scent of incense and aged wood. Shadows stretched across the walls, creating a dance of light and dark that felt oddly appropriate for the turmoil I'd carried inside for six years.

Ms. Vesper, the mysterious owner of the Arcane Room, sat behind a large oak desk at the far end of the room. As I approached, her dark eyes locked onto mine, seeing right through me, past the walls I'd carefully built up over the years.

"Welcome, Amelia," she said, her voice as smooth as silk, wrapping around me with an odd mix of comfort and unease. "What brings you here today?"

For a moment, I hesitated, my fingers instinctively reaching for the rainbow ribbon knotted around my car keys —a keepsake Flynn had given me so many years ago. It was a gift, something he'd braided himself, something that had once tied us together. The ribbon was frayed now, much like the connection between us. I took a deep breath, forcing myself to meet Ms. Vesper's gaze. "I want to remember," I said, the words trembling on my lips. "I want to remember what it was like with him—with Flynn. I need to understand why I can't let go. Because I *need* to let go."

Ms. Vesper nodded slowly, as if she'd expected this. "The heart clings to the past when it hasn't found peace in the present," she said softly. Her words hit me like a physical blow, a truth I'd tried to ignore for so long. "Memories are powerful things, Amelia. They can heal, but they can also hurt. Are you certain you're ready to confront them?"

I swallowed hard, the weight of her question pressing down on me. I'd spent years trying to forget, trying to move on, but no matter what I did, Flynn was always there, lingering in the corners of my mind. I was tired of running from the memories that refused to fade.

"Yes," I said, though my voice was more confident than I felt. "I'm ready."

Ms. Vesper gave me a small, approving smile and gestured to a velvet cushion on the floor in front of her desk. "Sit," she instructed. "We'll begin with the cards."

I did as she said, sinking onto the cushion, my heart pounding in my chest as I watched her reach for a deck of tarot cards. They looked old, the edges frayed, as if they'd been handled by countless people searching for answers. As Ms. Vesper began to shuffle the deck, the air in the room shifted, charged with an energy that hummed against my skin.

"Close your eyes," she said, her voice low and soothing. "Clear your mind, and when you're ready, draw a card."

I closed my eyes, focusing on the rhythm of my breathing. In and out. In and out. I tried to push aside the doubts and fears that had gnawed at me for years, but it was impossible. I focused on Flynn instead—on the way his smile used to light up my world, the warmth of his arms around me, the way he made me feel alive like no one else ever could. Slowly, I reached out, my fingers brushing against the smooth surface of the cards. There was a subtle pull, an invisible force guiding me to a single card. I drew it from the deck and opened my eyes.

The Six of Cups.

My breath caught in my throat, and I stared at the card. Two children stood in a garden, exchanging flowers with a look of pure innocence and joy. The image stirred something deep inside me, a bittersweet ache that made my chest tighten.

Ms. Vesper took the card from my trembling hands, her smile deepening. "The Six of Cups," she murmured, her voice filled with understanding. "The Six of Cups is about memories, about the past, about first loves and the longing for what once was. It's about revisiting the past, about remembering the joys and the sorrows of love lost. It speaks to the purity of first love, of childhood memories that linger long after they've passed. It's a perfect choice for what you seek."

I could only nod, unable to find my voice as I continued to stare at the card. It felt like the universe itself had chosen it for me, knowing exactly what I needed to see, what I needed to confront.

Ms. Vesper rose from her chair and moved to a small cabinet behind her desk. She retrieved a teacup and set it in front of me. With a fluid motion, she poured hot water into the cup, the steam rising in delicate tendrils. She handed it to me, and my hands shook as I took it, the weight of what I was about to do settling heavily on my shoulders.

"This tea will guide you through the Arcane Room's most powerful experience," Ms. Vesper explained, her eyes never leaving mine. "A simulation that will allow you to relive your memories as if you were there again. It will be intense, and it will be real. But remember, Amelia, what you see in the simulation is a reflection of your own heart. It's up to you to find the meaning in it."

I nodded, my throat too tight to speak. My mind raced with questions, but I knew that no answer Ms. Vesper could give me would ease the anxiety twisting in my gut. "What do I do?" I managed to whisper.

"Follow me," she said, leading me to a back room. When we entered, it was stark white, with a black leather chaise lounge. "Drink the tea and relax here," she said, gesturing to the couch. "Once you finish your tea, the simulation will begin."

I glanced at the door, then back at Ms. Vesper. Her calm demeanor was reassuring, but it didn't stop the tremor in my hands as I brought the tea to my lips. The liquid was bitter, and I fought the urge to spit it out as it slid down my throat.

Ms. Vesper's eyes softened, and she reached out to squeeze my hand. "Good luck, Amelia. And remember, no matter how much time you think has passed, it will only be twenty minutes."

With that, I sat on the chaise, my heart pounding a drumbeat of anticipation. I took one last deep breath and closed my eyes.

The world shifted around me, and I was no longer in the Arcane Room—I stood on the beach, the warm sand beneath my bare feet, the sound of waves crashing against the shore filling my senses.

And there, standing just a few feet away, was Flynn.

He was exactly as I remembered him at eighteen—tousled brown hair, a crooked smile that always made my heart race, and those piercing blue eyes that seemed to see right through me. My breath hitched as I took him in, my heart aching with a longing I hadn't allowed myself to feel in years.

Flynn's gaze locked onto mine, and the air between us thickened with an electricity I could almost taste. He didn't just look at me; he devoured me with those eyes, the kind of look that made my pulse quicken and heat bloom low in my belly. His lips curved into that infuriatingly sexy grin, the one that always spelled trouble. "Hey, Amelia," he drawled, his voice like honeyed whiskey—smooth, warm, and utterly intoxicating. "You ready?"

I swallowed hard, my throat suddenly dry, and managed a nod. Words failed me as he reached out and took my hand. The simple touch sent a jolt of awareness straight through me, lighting up every nerve ending. His hand was warm and solid, his grip just firm enough to remind me that this was real—that he was real. My heart pounded in my chest, echoing the beat of the waves crashing against the shore as he led me down the beach.

Every step we took together brought memories crashing over me—our first kiss under the stars, the way his lips claimed mine with a hunger that left me breathless, the nights we spent tangled up in each other, lost in a world that was ours alone. The longing I'd buried deep inside clawed its way to the surface, and I couldn't help but wonder if he felt it too —this undeniable pull, this gravitational force that always drew us back together.

Flynn stopped suddenly, and I nearly stumbled into him. He turned to face me, his gaze intense, searching my face as if trying to read the secrets hidden there. "I've got something for you," he murmured, reaching into his pocket. His voice was husky, laced with something darker, more dangerous, that made my pulse skitter wildly. When he pulled out the small, braided ribbon, my breath caught in my throat.

It was the same rainbow ribbon I'd kept knotted around my car keys since the day it fell off my wrist six years ago. But in his hands, it wasn't just a ribbon—it was a lifeline to the past, to everything we'd once shared. He held it out to me, his expression soft and vulnerable, yet there was a fire in his eyes that told me he wasn't just here to relive old memories. "I made this for you," he said, his voice low and rough, "so you'd always remember what it was like to be here, right now. So you'd remember us."

I stared at the ribbon, my heart twisting painfully as the weight of his words sank in. Our fingers brushed as I took it from him, and the contact sent a shiver down my spine. It wasn't just a touch—it was a promise, a challenge, a dare. The air between us was charged with a tension that was almost unbearable, and I could feel the heat of his body, so close, too close.

"I'll never forget," I whispered, my voice trembling with the force of everything I wasn't saying—everything I wanted, needed, but couldn't bring myself to admit. The waves roared in the background, but all I could hear was the pounding of my heart, the rush of blood in my ears.

Flynn's smile widened, but it wasn't boyish anymore. It was dark, wicked, and filled with a desire that mirrored my own. He stepped closer, so close that I could feel the warmth of his breath on my skin. His eyes flicked down to my lips, and I saw the decision in his gaze an instant before he moved.

His hand came up to cradle the back of my head, his fingers tangling in my hair, and then his mouth was on mine. The kiss wasn't gentle—it was fierce, possessive, claiming. It was everything I'd missed, everything I'd wanted, and it ignited a fire inside me that threatened to consume us both. Flynn kissed me like he was starving, like he'd been waiting years for this moment, and I kissed him back just as desperately.

My hands found his chest, the solid planes of muscle beneath his shirt, and I fisted the fabric, pulling him closer, needing him closer. The world around us faded away, leaving just the two of us, tangled together in a kiss that was anything but innocent. His teeth grazed my bottom lip, and I gasped, the sensation sending a thrill of pleasure straight to my core.

He groaned low in his throat, the sound vibrating through me, and deepened the kiss, his tongue sweeping into my mouth in a way that made my knees go weak. I clung to him, lost in the taste of him, the feel of him, the undeniable truth that this—this—was where I was meant to be. Where I'd always belonged.

When we finally broke apart, we were both breathing hard, our foreheads pressed together, our bodies still entwined. His thumb brushed across my cheek, a tender contrast to the wild heat that still burned between us. "Amelia," he whispered, his voice raw and filled with something that made my heart stutter. "I've missed you. God, I've missed you."

I looked up into his eyes, and in that moment, I knew—no matter how much time had passed, no matter how much had changed between us, this was far from over. The past might have torn us apart, but this kiss, this connection—it was the beginning of something new, something we couldn't ignore.

Two

Flynn's fingers lingered on my cheek, his touch warm and familiar, yet something was different. There was a strange light in his eyes, a depth I couldn't quite place. I pulled back slightly, searching his face for answers to the questions swirling in my mind.

"Flynn," I began, my voice wavering with uncertainty, "is this really you?"

He smiled, a small, wistful smile that tugged at the corners of his mouth. "I'm the memory of him, Amelia. Everything you experience here, it's all from your memories —your truths. I'm here because you wanted to see me, to remember."

The words hit me like a wave, washing over me with a strange mix of comfort and confusion. The Flynn standing before me wasn't just a figment of my imagination; he was a part of me, a piece of my past that I'd clung to for so long. And yet, there was something disorienting about it all, like standing on the edge of a dream you're not sure you want to wake from.

"You came to this place for a reason," Flynn continued, his voice soft but insistent. "You came to remember."

My breath caught in my throat as I thought back to the moment we'd just relived—the moment that had always been seared into my heart, the moment that had changed everything. "That was the moment I fell in love with you," I whispered, the confession spilling from my lips before I could stop it.

Flynn's eyes softened, a shadow of longing passing through them. "I've loved you longer," he said simply, his words carrying the weight of a truth I hadn't been ready to hear.

I shook my head, trying to resist the pull of his charm, the intensity of his gaze. "I can't know that," I protested, my voice trembling with the effort to keep my emotions in check. "How could I have known?"

"You did know it, Amelia," Flynn insisted, stepping closer, his presence overwhelming in its familiarity. "This place—it's made from your truths, your memories. It's designed to help you remember all the things you forgot, the things you tried to bury. You knew how I felt, even if you couldn't admit it to yourself."

His words echoed in my mind, each one digging deeper into the walls I'd built around my heart. It was as if he was peeling back the layers of my defenses, exposing the raw, vulnerable truth beneath. And the truth was, I had known. I'd always known.

"What's next?" I asked, my voice barely a whisper. The question hung in the air between us, heavy with anticipation, with the weight of everything we had yet to uncover.

Flynn's smile returned, a mixture of tenderness and something darker, something that hinted at the depths we had yet to explore. "I want to show you something."

Before I could respond, the world around us shimmered and shifted, the beach dissolving into a blur of colors and sounds. When the world reappeared, we were standing in front of a small, run-down house, the paint peeling from the walls, the windows dirty and cracked. The air was thick with tension, the kind that made the hairs on the back of my neck stand on end.

Standing just outside the house was a young girl—me, I realized with a jolt. I couldn't have been more than seven or eight years old, my hair in pigtails, my wide eyes filled with a mix of curiosity and fear. I watched as my younger self peered around the corner of the house, her gaze fixed on the scene unfolding in the front yard.

There, standing in the yard, was a young boy—Flynn. His hair was messy, his clothes dirty and too big for him, and his expression was one of pure terror. In front of him stood a man, his face twisted in anger, his hand raised as he screamed at Flynn, his voice filled with venom.

The man's hand came down hard, striking Flynn across the face. The sound of the slap echoed through the yard, and I saw Flynn stumble back, tears streaming down his cheeks. My younger self flinched, her hands trembling as she watched Flynn turn and run, his small form disappearing down the street.

I felt a wave of nausea wash over me as I remembered that day, the helplessness, the fear that had gripped me as I watched the boy I didn't even know get hurt. I had wanted to do something, to stop the man, but I'd been too afraid, too small to make a difference. Instead, I'd run home, my heart pounding with guilt and fear, the image of Flynn's tear-streaked face burned into my memory.

"That was the first time you ever saw me," Flynn said, his voice soft, almost reverent. "That man—he was my mother's boyfriend. He wasn't a good man. I was just a kid, but I knew enough to be afraid of him."

I swallowed hard, the guilt from that day resurfacing, choking me with its intensity. "I was afraid for you," I admitted, my voice barely audible. "But I didn't know your name. I was too afraid of him to do anything."

Flynn nodded, his expression filled with understanding. "And it was the next day when Jake and I were outside playing and broke your mother's favorite vase. You spoke up for me, Amelia. You convinced your mom it was your fault, that it was an accident, not mine. You saved me that day."

I shook my head, tears welling up in my eyes. "No, I didn't. It was just a vase."

But Flynn's eyes bore into mine, filled with a conviction that made my heart ache. "Yes, you did. If you hadn't spoken up, if you hadn't convinced her it wasn't my fault, she would have called my mom. And if she had called my mom, her boyfriend would have found out. He would have beaten me for it. You saved me from something horrible that day."

I felt a tear slip down my cheek, the weight of his words crushing me. I had never known the full extent of what I had done that day, never realized how much Flynn had been suffering. "I fell in love with you in that moment," Flynn continued, his voice thick with raw emotion. "I've loved you for nearly our entire lives."

"We were just kids," I whispered, my heart breaking at the realization of how deep his feelings had run, how much I had meant to him, even then.

"I know," Flynn said, his voice filled with a quiet strength. "And you were always saving me from a life I couldn't control."

I closed my eyes, letting his words wash over me, feeling the truth of them settle deep within me. This place—the Arcane Room—was showing me the things I had forgotten, the truths I had buried so deep that I had convinced myself they didn't exist. But they did exist, and they were more real than anything I had allowed myself to believe.

When I opened my eyes again, Flynn was watching me, his expression soft, filled with a love that spanned years, decades, lifetimes. And in that moment, I knew that no matter what came next, no matter how painful the memories might be, I had to face them. I had to remember.

Because in remembering, I could finally begin to heal.

Three

T he world around us shimmered and shifted once more, the memory of that painful day in Flynn's childhood fading away as the Arcane Room brought forth another moment from our past. When the mist cleared, I found myself back in my parents' backyard, the scent of freshly cut grass filling the air, and the gentle creak of the old hammock swaying in the summer breeze.

Flynn and I were twelve years old, lying side by side in the hammock, our legs dangling over the edge as we lazily rocked back and forth. I could almost feel the warmth of the sun on my skin, the simple joy of a summer day when everything felt easy and free. But as I watched the scene unfold, I knew that this memory wasn't as carefree as it appeared.

Flynn turned his head to look at my younger self, a soft smile playing on his lips. "You ever heard the story of Cassiopeia?" he asked, his voice light, but with an edge of excitement that made me smile even now.

My younger self shook her head, eyes wide with curiosity. "No, what's that?"

Flynn pointed up at the sky, even though the stars weren't out yet. "Cassiopeia is a constellation. It's shaped like a W or an M, depending on how you look at it. The story goes that Cassiopeia was this beautiful queen, but she was also really vain. She boasted that she was more beautiful than the sea nymphs, and that made Poseidon, the god of the sea, super mad. So he punished her by placing her in the sky, tied to her throne, where she'd spin around forever, sometimes upside down."

"Why upside down?" young Amelia asked, her voice a mix of wonder and concern.

"To teach her a lesson," Flynn explained, his tone softening. "To remind her that beauty isn't everything, and that sometimes, pride can get you into trouble."

My younger self considered this for a moment, then asked, "Do you think she ever got lonely up there, all by herself?"

Flynn's smile faltered slightly, his gaze turning more thoughtful. "Maybe. But I think she was probably more sad that she couldn't be with the people she loved anymore, you know? Being alone is one thing, but being apart from the people who matter... that's the real punishment."

I felt a pang in my chest at his words, the truth of them resonating even now. Flynn's gaze lingered on young Amelia, and I saw the way his expression softened, his eyes filled with something deeper, something he probably didn't even understand at that age. He leaned in closer, his breath warm on her cheek.

I watched, my heart aching for the girl I once was, for the boy who was about to take a step that could change everything.

Flynn hesitated, his lips just inches from hers, when suddenly, Jake's voice cut through the air like a sharp knife.

"Amelia!"

She jerked back, startled, and Flynn quickly pulled away, his face flushing with a mix of embarrassment and frustration. Jake stormed across the yard, his expression dark with anger as he glared at both of us.

"What are you doing?" Jake demanded, his voice accusatory, his eyes narrowed at Flynn.

"We were just talking," I said defensively, sitting up in the hammock, but Jake wasn't listening.

"You're always with her!" Jake snapped, his anger now fully directed at Flynn. "You're supposed to be my friend, not hers! You can't be both!"

Flynn looked between me and Jake, his expression torn, feeling the weight of Jake's ultimatum. I could see the conflict in his eyes, the struggle between loyalty to his best friend and the growing feelings he had for me.

In the end, Flynn made his choice.

He stood up from the hammock, his gaze dropping to the ground as he walked over to Jake. "I'm sorry, Amelia," he whispered, not daring to look at me as he turned and walked away with my brother.

That memory cut deep, the pain of rejection washing over me like it had all those years ago. Young Amelia sat in the hammock, watching them leave, tears welling up in her eyes as Flynn turned back, just for a moment, and mouthed, "Sorry."

But his apology didn't quell the hurt, didn't stop the feeling of abandonment that crushed my young heart. In that instant, I made a decision—a decision to never give Flynn the time of day again, to protect myself from the pain of caring for someone who could so easily walk away.

The scene faded, and the Arcane Room brought me back to Flynn's side.

"I was afraid, Amelia," Flynn said, his voice tinged with regret. "Afraid of losing Jake as a friend, afraid of losing your home as a safe place. I didn't know what else to do."

"I was crushed," I admitted, my voice thick with emotion. "I thought you only saw me as Jake's little sister."

Flynn shook his head, his eyes filled with a deep sorrow. "You were always more than that, Amelia. You've always been special to me."

"I spent weeks avoiding you," I confessed. "I was too embarrassed to face you after that."

"I know," Flynn said softly. "I spent weeks looking for you around every corner, hoping to see you, only to be disappointed when you weren't there."

I felt a lump form in my throat, the memories of those days swirling around me, the lost opportunities, the words left unsaid. "What's next?" I asked, needing to move forward, to understand the full picture of what we had lost and what we could possibly regain.

Flynn gave me a small, almost sad smile before the world shimmered again, and we found ourselves at a crowded outdoor film festival. The air was cool with the hint of autumn, the sky a deep indigo as the first stars began to peek through. I stood in line for popcorn, my arms wrapped around myself as I waited for my turn.

I remembered this night vividly. I was on a date with Thomas, a boy from school who had asked me out after months of flirting. He was saving our seats on the hay bales with a warm blanket made just for two, while I braved the concession line. I was nervous, excited for what the night might bring.

And then I saw him.

Flynn was working the popcorn stand, his face lighting up with surprise and something else when he spotted me. His grin was wide, genuine, but I could only remember the way my stomach dropped with embarrassment when our eyes met.

"Amelia," he said, his voice filled with a warmth that I hadn't expected, "are you on a date?"

"Yes," I'd replied, trying to keep my voice steady, but I

could feel the flush creeping up my neck. "Thomas is waiting for me."

Flynn's smile faltered slightly, his gaze flicking towards where I assumed Thomas was sitting. "The hotshot wannabe firefighter can't afford popcorn? He's making you pay for the concessions?" Flynn asked, a note of incredulity in his voice. "It's a free movie. Some kind of date that is."

I bristled at his tone, crossing my arms over my chest defensively. "I'm a powerful, independent woman, Flynn. I don't need help from anyone. Not even my date, and especially not from you."

Flynn raised an eyebrow, clearly amused by my response, but he didn't push further. He handed me the popcorn, his fingers brushing mine for the briefest moment. "Enjoy your date, Amelia."

I turned away, my heart pounding, and made my way back to Thomas, who was waiting with a disinterested expression. As I sat down beside him, my mind kept drifting back to Flynn, to the way he had looked at me, the way his smile had faltered when I mentioned Thomas.

"You know," I said, breaking the silence between us, "I remember being annoyed that I had to pay for the whole date. Thomas was the one who asked me out, and then he conveniently forgot his wallet."

Flynn chuckled softly, the sound vibrating through me, warming me in ways Thomas never could. "I remember. I watched you the whole night, Amelia. Wishing I was there instead of him. Wishing that I could wrap my arms around you and keep you warm. Wishing that you were mine."

His words sent a shiver down my spine, the intensity of his longing seeping into every corner of my being. I turned to look at him, my breath catching in my throat as his gaze locked onto mine, filled with a desire that was impossible to ignore.

Flynn reached out, his fingers gently brushing my cheek, his touch sending a jolt of electricity through me. The space between us crackled with tension, the air thick with the unspoken feelings that had been building for years. I could feel my resolve crumbling, the walls I had built around my heart slowly giving way under the weight of everything I had tried to deny.

"Flynn," I whispered, my voice trembling with the force of my emotions.

He leaned in closer, his breath warm against my lips, his eyes searching mine for any sign of hesitation. But there was none. I couldn't stop myself, couldn't fight the pull that had always existed between us.

And so, I kissed him.

The moment our lips met, the world dissolved, leaving just the two of us, tangled together in a kiss that was filled with all the longing, all the desire, all the love that had been simmering beneath the surface for so long. Flynn's hands slipped around my waist, pulling me closer, deepening the kiss as if he was afraid to let go.

I melted into him, my heart racing, my mind spinning with the realization that this—this—was what I had been missing. This was what I had been searching for, even when I didn't know it.

When we finally broke apart, we were both breathless, our foreheads pressed together as we tried to catch our breath. Flynn's eyes were dark, filled with a longing that matched my own.

But as much as I wanted to stay in that moment forever, I knew that there were still more memories to uncover, more truths to face.

"What's next?" I whispered, my voice barely audible, but Flynn heard me. He always did.

And with a gentle smile, he led me into the next memory, leaving the taste of his kiss lingering on my lips, a promise of everything that was yet to come.

Four

The world shimmered and shifted once more, and when it settled, I found myself sitting in the passenger seat of Flynn's old, beat-up car. The familiar scent of the worn leather seats mixed with the crisp ocean air wafting through the open windows, and I could almost feel the excitement bubbling up inside me as I relived the memory.

It was our first real date, a drive from Coral Cove to Forks. I had just finished devouring the *Twilight* books, caught up in the whirlwind romance and the supernatural sparkle that had taken over my imagination. Flynn, always the one to make me smile, had promised me a day full of fun and surprises, and I couldn't wait to see what he had in store.

We were nearing Forks when Flynn pulled into a small roadside stop, claiming he needed to use the bathroom. I remember the way he had winked at me, a mischievous glint in his eyes, before hopping out of the car and disappearing into the small building.

I waited in the car, my mind wandering as I admired the towering evergreens that lined the road, the thick moss draping the trunks like nature's own velvet. The excitement of the day thrummed in my veins, and I found myself daydreaming about the possibilities, about what might happen next.

When Flynn finally emerged, my breath caught in my throat. The sunlight streaming through the trees caught on his skin, and he…sparkled. Just like Edward in *Twilight*.

For a moment, I was stunned into silence. But then, a burst of laughter escaped my lips, the sound echoing through the car as I took in the sight of him, covered in glitter, shining like the vampire from my favorite book.

Flynn struck a pose, his arms outstretched, a grin spreading across his face. "Well?" he asked, his voice filled with playful anticipation. "Do I dazzle you, Miss Swan?"

I couldn't stop laughing, tears forming in the corners of my eyes. "Flynn, you're ridiculous," I managed to say between giggles. "Never stop being silly."

He stepped closer, leaning down so that our faces were just inches apart. "I'll never stop making you smile," he promised, his voice softening, the humor giving way to something sweeter, something deeper.

And then, he kissed me.

The kiss was sweet, filled with the tenderness of a first date, the kind of kiss that made your heart flutter and your knees weak. It was the perfect moment, the kind of moment I had always dreamed of, and I melted into him, my laughter fading into a soft sigh of contentment.

As the memory fast-forwarded, the scene shifted to later in the day. We were sitting on the beach, the sound of the waves crashing against the shore providing a soothing backdrop to the warmth of Flynn's arms wrapped around me. He was behind me, holding me close, his chin resting on my shoulder as we stared out at the horizon.

It was one of those moments where everything felt right, where the world seemed to slow down, and all that mattered was the person next to you. We had talked for hours, sharing our hopes and dreams, the kind of dreams that felt so close, yet still just out of reach.

"I got into the University of Washington," Flynn said, his voice quiet, almost hesitant. "And Western Washington University."

I turned to face him, my eyes wide with excitement. "Flynn, that's amazing! I'm so happy for you!"

He smiled, a little bashful, but there was pride in his eyes. "I'm still waiting to hear back from a few others, but those are my top two. What about you? Any letters yet?"

I shook my head, a small frown tugging at my lips. "Not yet, but I'm hopeful. No matter what, though, we're going together. We'll attend the same college."

Flynn's arms tightened around me, his voice filled with confidence. "You'll get in, Amelia. I know you will."

I leaned back into him, feeling the warmth of his body against mine, the steady beat of his heart beneath my ear. "I'm going to study film," I said, my voice soft as I shared my dream with him. "I've been obsessed with movies since I was little, ever since I first stepped into Rewind Rentals. I don't know if I want to make movies, but I want to study them, learn everything I can."

"You're going to be a famous film critic someday," Flynn said, his voice full of conviction. "People will listen to you. They'll care about what you have to say."

I smiled, a little shy, a little uncertain. "Maybe. But I'd be happy just running Rewind Rentals one day. I love that place. It's home."

Flynn kissed the top of my head, his lips warm against my skin. "Then that's what you'll do. And when I go into business, I'll help you make that dream come true."

The memory was so bittersweet, so filled with the promise of a future we'd never quite reach. As I relived it, my heart ached with the knowledge of how things had turned out, how life had taken us down different paths,

paths that didn't quite lead to the dreams we had shared that day.

As the memory faded, I turned to Flynn, the real Flynn—or at least, the memory of him. The ache in my chest was almost unbearable as I looked into his eyes, the eyes of the boy I had loved so deeply.

"I'm just starting to take over for my parents at the store," I confessed, my voice trembling with the weight of everything that had gone unsaid. "But it's so much harder than I ever imagined. I thought I'd feel at home there, but sometimes I feel so lost."

Flynn's gaze softened, filled with that unwavering belief he had always had in me. "I believe in you, Amelia. You're going to figure it out. You always do. All your dreams are coming true."

I shook my head, tears welling up in my eyes. "No, they didn't. Because you're not here. You left, Flynn. Why did you leave?"

Flynn sighed, a deep, heavy sound that seemed to echo through the room. But he didn't answer. Instead, he just looked at me with those eyes that held so much love, so much regret, that it made my heart feel like it was breaking all over again.

Five

nstead of pushing for an answer, the words caught in my throat, I did the only thing that felt right in that moment—I kissed him. But this wasn't a gentle, sweet kiss like the ones we'd shared in the past. No, this was a kiss fueled by years of longing, of missed opportunities, and unspoken desires. My hands tangled in Flynn's hair, pulling him closer, as if I could make him stay with me, make him real, if I just held on tight enough.

Flynn responded with equal fervor, his hands moving to my waist, pulling me flush against him. The air between us crackled with electricity, the tension that had been building since I stepped into the Arcane Room now snapping like a live wire. I broke the kiss only long enough to whisper, "I don't want to talk right now. I want you."

Something dark and intense flared in Flynn's eyes, and before I could catch my breath, he scooped me up into his arms. The world around us shifted, and suddenly, we were in a room I didn't recognize, a large bed with soft, rumpled sheets appearing out of nowhere. Flynn laid me down gently, his hands already moving to undress me, his touch igniting every nerve in my body.

We fumbled with each other's clothes, our hands eager, desperate, as if undressing was the only way to close the gap between us. Soon, I was lying naked before him, my skin tingling under his gaze. Flynn paused, his eyes raking over my body with an intensity that made my heart race.

"You're beautiful," he murmured, his voice thick with desire. He leaned down, brushing his lips over mine before pulling back just enough to look into my eyes. "I'm going to make you come, Amelia."

"Thank the goddess," I breathed, my body already aching for him.

Flynn smiled—a slow, wicked smile that sent a shiver of anticipation down my spine. He moved lower, pulling my legs up over his shoulders, and I felt the warmth of his breath against my most intimate parts. He didn't rush; instead, he took a moment to inhale deeply, as if savoring the scent of me.

"You're intoxicating," he said, his voice reverent, before lowering his mouth to my core.

The first touch of his tongue made me gasp, my hips jerking involuntarily. Flynn licked me from my cunt to my clit, his movements slow and deliberate, as if he wanted to draw out every ounce of pleasure he could. I moaned, the sound filling the room as he buried himself in my heat, his tongue exploring me with a thoroughness that made my head spin.

All the worries I had been carrying fell away, replaced by the overwhelming sensation of Flynn's mouth on me, his tongue working me with a skill that had my toes curling. My breaths came in short, ragged gasps, the heat coiling in my belly, tightening with every flick of his tongue.

He didn't let up, his hands gripping my thighs, holding me in place as he devoured me, his mouth working a relentless rhythm that had me teetering on the edge of release. I couldn't think, couldn't speak—only feel. And then, just when I thought I couldn't take any more, Flynn pulled back, his lips glistening, and gently set me down on the bed.

"Flynn," I begged, my voice thick with need, "please, fuck me."

He didn't need any more encouragement. Flynn positioned himself above me, his large, thick cock pressing against my entrance. He moved slowly, letting me feel every inch as he entered me, stretching me to accommodate him. The sensation was exquisite, a mix of pleasure and pressure that had me moaning in pure bliss.

Once he was fully seated inside me, he paused, allowing me a moment to adjust, his eyes never leaving mine. The connection between us was electric, the air thick with the shared knowledge that this was something we had both wanted for so long.

When Flynn finally began to move, it was slow and deliberate, each thrust sending a wave of pleasure rippling through my body. I moaned louder, my hands gripping his shoulders, digging my nails into his skin as I held on to him, feeling the tension building with every thrust.

"I want to feel inside you when you come," Flynn whispered, his voice ragged with restraint. "Is that okay?"

I nodded enthusiastically, my mind too clouded with pleasure to form words. Flynn's pace quickened, his thrusts coming faster, harder, each one driving me closer to the edge. He pulled out briefly, just long enough to wet his finger with my juices before thrusting back inside me again.

As he did, he moved that slick finger to my ass, slowly pressing against my puckered entrance. The sensation made me gasp, my body tensing at the unexpected but not unwelcome intrusion. Flynn was careful, moving slowly, letting me adjust as he entered me with both his cock and his finger.

The dual sensation was overwhelming, a mix of fullness and heat that had me writhing beneath him, my body reacting on instinct, craving more. Flynn picked up the pace, his thrusts becoming more urgent as he worked his finger deeper inside me, matching the rhythm of his cock.

My body tightened around him, the pleasure coiling in my belly, spiraling higher and higher until I felt like I was going to shatter. I dug my nails into his back, holding on to him as the final crash hit me, the orgasm ripping through me with such force that I lost my hearing for a moment, my vision going white.

Flynn didn't relent; he continued to fuck me through the aftershocks, his cock still buried deep inside me, his finger moving in tandem. The sensations were too much, too intense, but I didn't want him to stop—I wanted more, wanted to lose myself in the overwhelming pleasure of him.

I reached down, my fingers finding the bundle of nerves at my clit, and I began to rub, the quick, rhythmic pressure sending me spiraling into another orgasm. This time, Flynn came with me, his body tensing above mine as he released his own orgasm, filling me with his seed.

The warmth of his cum spread through me, a soothing balm that I relished, wanting every ounce of him inside me. For a brief moment, I forgot that this wasn't reality, that this was just a dream. In this dream, I could have all of him, and I wanted it all.

But as the pleasure ebbed, reality slowly crept back in. Flynn remained inside me, his breathing heavy, his body still trembling with the aftermath of our shared release. I wrapped my arms around him, holding him close, savoring the warmth of his skin against mine, the steady beat of his heart beneath my ear.

But it wasn't enough. It would never be enough. Because, in the end, this wasn't real.

And that truth, more than anything, left me aching for something I could never truly have.

$\mathcal{S}ix$

The room was quiet now, the echoes of our shared ecstasy still lingering in the air, mingling with the scent of sex and sweat. I lay there, Flynn's strong arms wrapped around me, feeling more at peace than I had in a long time. But even in this moment of bliss, a question lingered in the back of my mind, one that I wasn't sure I was ready to confront.

"Can I just stay here, like this, forever?" I whispered, my voice tinged with a vulnerability I couldn't hide.

Flynn's fingers gently traced patterns on my bare back, his touch soothing. "This is your space, Ams," he murmured, his voice low and tender. "We can stay like this for as long as you want. But eventually, you're going to want to know the rest. You came here for a reason."

His words were a reminder of the truth I was trying so hard to avoid, the truth that had brought me to the Arcane Room in the first place. But for now, all I wanted was to stay in this moment, to hold on to the fantasy a little longer.

"Can we go one more round before we face the inevitable?" I asked, a playful smile tugging at my lips.

Flynn's eyes darkened with desire, a low growl rumbling

in his chest. "Only if I can tie you up and have my way with you."

The thought alone sent a surge of arousal coursing through me, liquid heat pooling between my legs at the idea of giving myself over to him completely. It was something I had dreamed of for so long, but the real Flynn had never ventured into that territory. Now, in this space where anything was possible, I wanted to experience it all.

"That's always been a fantasy of mine," I admitted, my voice hushed with anticipation.

Flynn's lips curved into a knowing smile. "You have to be more communicative with your desires. Speaking as Flynn, I know he would have enjoyed it."

I laughed, the sound light and filled with a sense of freedom. "You seem to know my desires just fine."

"Of course I do," he said, his voice deepening with promise. "This is your world, Amelia. We can get as naughty as you'd like here."

As if on cue, a pile of leather and nylon straps appeared on the bed beside us. There were cuffs too, and in the middle of the pile was a thigh restraint or I think I heard it once called a bondage spreader. It was a contraption that made my pulse race just looking at it. My eyes widened as I took it all in, my breath catching in my throat at the thought of being bound, helpless, completely at his mercy.

Flynn's fingers trailed down my arm, leaving goosebumps in their wake. "Do you trust me?" he asked, his voice low and serious.

"With everything I have," I whispered.

He smiled, that dark, wicked smile that made my insides melt. "Then let's make this dream of yours come true."

With practiced hands, Flynn began to secure the restraints, slipping my legs into the cuffs that hooked at my thighs. The sensation of being bound, of having my movements restricted, sent a shiver of anticipation through me. Next, he wrapped the strap around my back, securing my wrists in the cuffs, leaving me spread eagle, utterly vulnerable, my cunt on full display for him.

He stepped back, his gaze raking over my body, and I could see the hunger in his eyes, the need to claim me, to take me in ways I had only ever fantasized about.

"You look incredible," Flynn said, his voice thick with desire. He reached into the pile of toys and pulled out a small, vibrating egg. My breath hitched as he brought it closer, teasing me.

He didn't rush. Instead, he let the anticipation build, holding the vibrating egg just above my clit, letting it buzz in the air, sending waves of pleasure rippling through me even without direct contact. I moaned, my body arching off the bed, desperate for more.

Finally, Flynn lowered the egg, pressing it against my clit, and a jolt of pleasure shot through me, so intense that I couldn't stop the cry that escaped my lips. He circled the egg around my clit, teasing me, driving me to the brink, only to pull back just when I thought I might explode.

"Please," I whimpered, my voice barely more than a breath. "I need more."

Flynn's smile widened, a devilish glint in his eyes. "You'll get more, Ams. So much more."

He moved the egg lower, slipping it inside me with agonizing slowness, licking me before sliding it as deep as his fingers would allow. The vibrations inside me were maddening, the sensation of being filled, teased, and denied all at once making my head spin.

I was lost in the pleasure, my body trembling, when Flynn reached into the pile again and pulled out a set of nipple clamps. My eyes grew wide, a mix of fear and excitement coursing through me. I had never experimented with anything like this, but there was no one I trusted more than Flynn.

"You have such beautiful breasts," Flynn murmured, his voice a low purr as he leaned down, his breath hot against my skin. "Your nipples are so perky, your areolas a perfect pink. I want you to feel the most pleasure possible."

He placed the first clamp on my right nipple, the sharp pinch of it sending a shock of pleasure-pain straight to my core. I gasped, the sensation overwhelming, but not unwelcome. Flynn's tongue flicked out, licking the pinched area, and I moaned, the pleasure doubling as the vibration inside me continued its relentless assault.

When he placed the second clamp on my left nipple, I was nearly sent over the edge, the dual sensations threatening to tear me apart. My body was on fire, every nerve ending lit up, every sensation amplified by the restraints, by the helplessness, by the trust.

"I'm going to come," I gasped, the words tumbling out of me, desperate, pleading.

"Not yet, baby," Flynn growled, his voice thick and controlled. He positioned himself between my legs, his cock hard and ready, and in one smooth motion, he thrust into me, filling me completely.

Stars exploded behind my eyes, the orgasm tearing through me with a force that left me breathless, my entire body convulsing with the intensity of it. But Flynn didn't stop. He kept moving, his cock driving in and out of me, his finger playing at the puckered entrance of my rosebud, the clamps on my nipples heightening every sensation.

Another orgasm built, faster this time, the buzzing inside me, the hard thrusts of his cock, the tight pinch of the clamps combining into a symphony of pleasure that had me screaming his name. And when the second orgasm hit, it was even more powerful than the first, my body tightening around him, pulling him deeper as I came again, harder, louder.

Flynn followed me over the edge, his own release shuddering through him as he emptied himself inside me, filling me with his seed. The warmth of it spread through me, soothing, calming, and I relished every second of it, holding on to him as the waves of pleasure slowly ebbed.

When it was over, Flynn carefully unhooked the restraints, his hands gentle as he freed me. He gathered me in his arms, cradling me against his chest, his fingers brushing through my hair as we lay there, our breathing slowly returning to normal.

This moment, this feeling of safety and belonging, of being utterly cherished, was everything I had ever wanted. But even as I lay there in Flynn's arms, I knew that this wasn't reality. It was a beautiful, perfect dream, but one that couldn't last forever.

And as much as I wanted to stay in this dream, to hold on to him and never let go, I knew that eventually, I would have to face the truth. The real world was waiting, with all its messiness and pain, and I couldn't hide in this fantasy forever.

Seven

The warmth of Flynn's embrace lingered even as the world around us began to shift once more. I knew it was time to face the things I had been avoiding, the memories I had come here to confront. Flynn and I untangled from the bed, the air still thick with the echoes of our passion. I took a deep breath, steeling myself for whatever came next.

Flynn watched me closely, his eyes filled with understanding and something that looked like sorrow. "Are you ready?" he asked, his voice gentle, as if he knew how much this was going to hurt.

I nodded, though my heart clenched at the thought. "I'm ready."

The room around us shimmered, the bed fading away as the Arcane Room brought forth a memory I had buried deep, one that was so sweet it was almost painful to recall. When the mist cleared, we were back in my old bedroom, the familiar surroundings bringing a rush of nostalgia. The walls were painted a soft lavender, the bedspread a patchwork quilt my mother had made. Everything was just as it had been all those years ago.

And there, on the bed, were two younger versions of

ourselves—Flynn and I, both nervous, both eager, about to share something incredibly special.

It was our first time.

I watched as we fumbled through the initial awkwardness, our hands tentative, our touches uncertain. But even in our inexperience, there was a tenderness between us, a connection that made everything feel right. Flynn was so good with me, so gentle and giving, always making sure I was comfortable, that I was ready. We laughed a lot, the nervous energy between us dissipating with every shared smile, every soft kiss.

Flynn's hands were warm as they trailed over my skin, his lips following in their wake. He took his time, never rushing, always checking in with me, making sure I was okay. It was sweet and romantic, everything I had ever hoped for. And when he finally entered me, it was with such care, such love, that the pain was barely noticeable. Instead, all I felt was the overwhelming sense of being cherished, of being loved.

Afterward, we lay tangled together in the sheets, our bodies still flush with the warmth of our lovemaking. Flynn's arm was draped over my waist, his fingers lazily tracing circles on my skin. I was curled into his side, my head resting on his chest, listening to the steady beat of his heart.

"I love you, Amelia," Flynn whispered, his voice soft, filled with sincerity. It was the first time he had said those words, and they filled the room with a warmth that seemed to seep into every corner of my soul.

"I love you too, Flynn," I whispered back, my heart swelling with the enormity of what we had just shared.

As I watched the memory play out, a bittersweet smile tugged at my lips. "It was the most perfect first time," I said softly, my voice filled with the weight of nostalgia. "Something straight out of a book. Unlike my girlfriends, I got lucky with you, Flynn."

Flynn, standing beside me, gave me a soft smile, his eyes filled with affection. "I got lucky with you too, Ams."

The memory faded, the warmth of that perfect moment slowly giving way to something else, something less certain, less happy. The world around us shifted, and when it settled again, we were in a long corridor, the bustling sounds of college students filling the air. The familiar scent of freshly brewed coffee mixed with the smell of textbooks and lecture halls. I knew exactly where we were—Western Washington University, the place where our dreams had started to take shape.

Flynn and I were walking down the corridor, our hands intertwined as we talked about the future, about what would happen after college. We had both gotten into Western, just like we had dreamed. Flynn was studying business, and I was studying film, just as we had planned. We were living the dream, or so it seemed.

"I was thinking," Flynn said, his voice bright with excitement, "after we graduate, maybe we could get a place together in the city. Seattle's got so much to offer—business opportunities for me, film festivals for you. It'd be perfect."

I smiled, though there was a hint of hesitation in it. "That sounds amazing, but... I was thinking maybe we could move back to Coral Cove. I love it there, and Rewind Rentals... well, it's home. I've always dreamed of running the place someday."

The conversation faltered, an awkward silence stretching between us as we realized, in that moment, that our visions of the future were different. We had always been so in sync, but now, for the first time, there was a disconnect, a small fissure that neither of us knew how to bridge.

Flynn looked at me, his expression uncertain. "The city could be a great adventure, Ams. There's so much out there. Don't you want to explore it?"

"I do," I said, my voice softer now, more contemplative.

"But Coral Cove... it's where I see us settling down. It's where our roots are."

The uncomfortable exchange hung in the air between us, unresolved, as Flynn glanced at his watch. "I have to get to class," he said, almost too quickly, as if eager to escape the tension. "We'll talk more later, okay?"

I nodded, forcing a smile. "Yeah, sure."

And just like that, he was gone, leaving me standing alone in the corridor, a sinking feeling in my chest. It was a small moment, but it was the first sign that something wasn't quite right. The first crack in the foundation of what we had built together.

As the memory faded, I turned to the Flynn standing beside me, the older, more knowing version of the boy I had loved. "This is where it all started to go wrong," I said quietly, my voice tinged with regret. "It wasn't quite the same after that, was it?"

Flynn sighed, his expression filled with the same sadness that I felt. "No, it wasn't. We had different dreams, different paths we wanted to take. And we didn't know how to reconcile that."

I nodded, the weight of those years pressing down on me, the realization that we had drifted apart without even knowing it. We had been so young, so sure that love would be enough to keep us together, to make everything work. But sometimes, love wasn't enough.

And that truth, more than anything, was the hardest to accept.

Eight

The air in the Arcane Room grew heavier, thick with the weight of what was left unsaid between us. I turned to Flynn, the tears I had been holding back finally spilling over as I let out a shaky breath.

"When we realized we had different visions of the future, I fell apart," I admitted, my voice trembling. "I spiraled, Flynn. I kept thinking, 'How could we want different futures? How could we love each other so much and not want the same things?' It made me doubt everything—us, our love, even myself. I wondered if you didn't love me enough or if maybe I didn't love you enough."

Flynn's gaze softened, his expression filled with regret. "It was never so cut and dry, Ams," he said quietly. "It wasn't about love. We just... we were so young, and we didn't know how to handle it. How to talk about it."

The room shimmered and shifted, and when the world settled again, I was sitting at Flynn's desk in his college dorm room. The familiar clutter of textbooks, notebooks, and coffee mugs surrounded me, the scent of his cologne lingering in the air. Flynn stood by the door, his keys in hand, flashing me that crooked smile that always made my heart skip a beat.

"I'm just going to use the restroom, and then we can head out," he said.

I smiled back at him, nodding. "Okay."

As he left the room, I glanced around, my eyes catching on a piece of paper partially hidden under a stack of books. Curious, I reached over and pulled it out, my breath catching in my throat as I read the words on the page.

It was an offer letter—from a business firm in Seattle.

I felt like the air had been sucked out of the room. My chest tightened, my heart pounding as I tried to process what I was seeing. We had been avoiding the conversation about our future, about what would happen after graduation, but it looked like Flynn had already made up his mind. Without me.

Anger, hurt, and a deep sense of betrayal surged through me all at once. How could he make this decision without even talking to me? I felt the sting of tears in my eyes, but I refused to let them fall. Instead, I did the one thing I regret more than anything.

I left.

I walked out of his room without a word, not waiting for him to return. I didn't want to confront him, didn't want to hear whatever excuses he might have had. I wanted to protect my heart, to shield myself from the pain of knowing that the boy I loved might be planning a future that didn't include me.

I avoided his calls, ignored his texts, and lied, telling him I was busy studying for finals. I built a wall around myself, hoping that if I kept him at arm's length, it wouldn't hurt so much when he inevitably left.

But even now, standing in the Arcane Room, I knew how wrong I had been. How much I regretted those choices.

"I should have been more firm," I whispered, my voice barely audible. "I should have told him what I thought, what I wanted. But I chickened out. I was so scared of losing him that I lost him anyway."

The room began to blur, the memory shifting as the world around us faded once more. When it came back into focus, we were at our college graduation. The ceremony was over, and the campus was buzzing with excitement as students and their families celebrated. Flynn and I stood together, slightly apart from the crowd, our caps and gowns marking the end of an era.

There was a moment, a brief, fragile moment where everything seemed to hang in the balance.

"I love you, Amelia," Flynn said, his voice filled with sincerity, with a kind of desperate hope.

I should have said it back. I wanted to say it back. But instead, the words that tumbled from my mouth were sharp, filled with the hurt and anger that had been festering inside me.

"I saw the offer letter in Seattle," I said, my voice cold, distant.

Flynn sighed, his shoulders sagging as he realized why I was upset. "It's just an offer," he said, trying to placate me. "There are lots of them."

"Lots of them?" I repeated, my brow furrowing. "What do you mean there are lots of them? I didn't even know you were putting feelers out there."

"That's not what I meant," Flynn said quickly, shaking his head. "Yes, there are a lot of offers. I've been networking for four years, Amelia. That was always the plan."

"The plan?" I echoed, my voice rising with disbelief. "My plan was always to go back to Coral Cove. I thought we were on the same page."

Flynn's expression softened, and he reached out to take my hand, but I pulled away. "Amelia, you're the love of my life," he said, his voice pleading, desperate. "None of this changes that. I love you more than anything."

But I couldn't bring myself to say it back. Not this time. The hurt ran too deep, the sense of betrayal too strong.

"When were you going to tell me about it?" I asked, my voice trembling with emotion.

"I planned on it after graduation," he said, running a hand through his tousled hair, frustration etched into every line of his face. "I just... I didn't want to add more stress before finals."

"Well, it's after graduation now," I said, my voice bitter.

Flynn hesitated, then finally said, "I've been given a really amazing opportunity, Amelia."

"I'm happy for you," I replied automatically, the words feeling hollow even as they left my lips.

Flynn looked at me, his eyes filled with disbelief. "Are you?"

I swallowed hard, feeling the tears welling up again. "I will never beg a man to love me or to choose me, Flynn. If this is what you want, then go. But don't expect me to wait for you."

And with that, I turned around and walked away.

The memory faded, tears streamed down my face. The pain of that day, the anguish of walking away from the person I loved most in the world, crashed over me like a wave. I couldn't hold it back any longer. He left us. He choose his career over me.

Flynn wrapped his arms around me, pulling me close as I sobbed against his chest. "I'm sorry, Amelia," he whispered, his voice thick with emotion. "It wasn't your fault. You were always clear about what you wanted, and I was always trying to figure out what I needed. Coral Cove held a lot of trauma for me, and I just wanted to escape it all. I wanted to do that with you, but I didn't consider your needs. I lied to myself, thinking that it would all just come together. It wasn't your fault, Amelia."

But I couldn't stop crying, the weight of my regrets, my choices, crushing me. "It was," I choked out. "I was awful to you. But I was hurt, Flynn. You kept me in the dark, and I didn't know how to deal with that."

Flynn pulled back, cupping my face in his hands, his eyes locking onto mine. "We all make choices, Ams. And we both made mistakes. But it wasn't your fault. We were young, and we didn't know how to handle it. But I never stopped loving you. Not for a second."

I let out a shuddering breath, the tears still falling, but the heaviness in my chest beginning to ease. "I never stopped loving you either," I whispered, my voice breaking.

Flynn held me tight, and for a moment, we just stood there, clinging to each other, letting the emotions wash over us. I felt a sense of peace start to settle in, the sharp edges of my regret slowly softening.

After a while, Flynn pulled back, looking at me with a tenderness that made my heart ache. "There's just one last memory to show you," he said softly.

I nodded, knowing that whatever came next, I was ready to face it. I had to. For both of us.

Nine

The world around us shimmered one last time, the memories of the past fading into a haze as the Arcane Room prepared to show me the final piece of the puzzle. I turned to Flynn, a question in my eyes as I tried to understand what was coming next.

"What is this about?" I asked, my voice barely above a whisper.

Flynn didn't answer right away. Instead, he nodded toward the scene unfolding in front of us. "Just watch," he said softly.

I took a deep breath and looked ahead. The room solidified around us, and I found myself walking through the door of the Arcane Room, just as I had done when this journey first began. But something was different this time. The air seemed heavier, charged with an energy that made my skin tingle.

As I walked deeper into the room, I noticed two women standing near the entrance, their voices low but distinct enough to carry to my ears.

"Did you hear that Flynn Callahan is moving back to town?" one of the women said, her tone laced with curiosity.

The other woman gasped, her eyes widening in surprise. "He is? I always wondered what he got up to after college."

I stopped in my tracks, the words hitting me like a freight train. I didn't remember this happening—at least, not in the way it was being shown to me now. My heart raced, and I turned to Flynn, my mind spinning with questions.

"Is it true?" I asked, my voice trembling with the weight of the possibility.

Flynn's eyes softened, and instead of answering, he pulled me close, his lips finding mine in a kiss so tender, so full of love, that it chased away every other thought. For that moment, there was no room for anything but him—the feel of his lips against mine, the warmth of his body pressed to me, the undeniable connection we had always shared.

When he finally pulled back, he rested his forehead against mine, his breath mingling with mine. "I love you, Amelia," he whispered, his voice filled with a deep, aching sincerity. "I always have. You're the love of my life."

Tears welled up in my eyes as I looked into his, the truth of his words resonating deep within me. "I love you too, Flynn. A part of me always has, even when I tried to convince myself otherwise."

He smiled, a bittersweet curve of his lips, and kissed me again, one last time. The kiss was everything—tender, passionate, a final goodbye that held all the emotions we had never been able to fully express. And as our lips parted, I felt a strange sense of peace settle over me, even as Flynn's form began to fade, the edges of his silhouette blurring until there was nothing left but the memory of his touch.

I blinked, and suddenly I was back in the Arcane Room, lying on the black leather chaise lounge. The room was still, the air heavy with the remnants of what I had just experienced. The tears I had been holding back finally broke free, streaming down my cheeks as the reality of it all crashed over me.

Ms. Vesper was there, her presence a calm, comforting force. She moved to sit next to me, wrapping her arms around me in a gentle embrace. "It's okay," she whispered, her voice a soothing to my wounded heart.

I leaned into her, letting the tears fall as she cradled me, the weight of everything I had been holding inside finally released. "Thank you," I choked out, my voice thick with emotion. "Thank you for letting me experience it one last time."

Ms. Vesper stroked my hair, her touch tender and reassuring. "You were ready, Amelia," she said softly. "Ready to move on, to let your heart heal. You're already living your best life, even if it doesn't feel that way right now."

I looked up at her, my tears starting to slow. "I want to believe that," I whispered.

Ms. Vesper smiled, a knowing, gentle smile that made me feel like everything would be okay. "The only person in life you can control is yourself. So be the best you, Amelia. Take what you can from the memories and know that life has a way of working out, even when we can't see how."

I nodded, feeling the truth in her words. I had spent so much time dwelling on the past, on what could have been, that I had forgotten to focus on the present, on the life I was building now.

As I stood to leave, I spotted the two women from the memory standing near the entrance of the Arcane Room. They were chatting animatedly, their voices blending with the soft hum of the room. I wondered briefly if they had actually talked about Flynn, if he really was moving back to town. But the thought passed quickly, replaced by something more important—what I needed now.

I had a family business to save, a life to live, and a heart that was finally ready to heal.

As I walked out of the Arcane Room and into the sunlight, I felt a strange sense of closure, of peace. I didn't know what the future held, but for the first time in a long time, I wasn't afraid. I was ready to face whatever came next, with the memory of Flynn in my heart, but not weighing me down.

And that was enough.

If you enjoyed the *Six of Cups*, and you want more of Amelia and Flynn's story, be sure to read:

LOVE REWOUND

Saving a store is one thing...
Saving their hearts is another.

Amelia:

Rewind Rentals is my family's legacy, but it's slipping away. When Flynn, the man who broke my heart, returns offering help, I'm torn between saving the store and risking my heart again.

Flynn:

I left Coral Cove to find success, but nothing compares to Amelia. Back to save Rewind Rentals, I'm determined to prove I've changed and win back the woman I never stopped loving.

In the small town of Coral Cove, Amelia Bennet is fighting to save Rewind Rentals, the last video rental store on the West Coast, from closing. The store, a nostalgic haven for film lovers, has been a part of her family for generations. With her parents ready to retire and the store struggling to stay afloat,

Amelia is determined to keep the doors open, even if it means taking on the challenges alone.

But when Flynn Callahan, her brother's best friend and the man who broke her heart six years ago, returns to town, everything changes. Flynn offers his expertise to help turn the business around, but the unresolved tension between them threatens to complicate their partnership. As they work together, mysterious and magical events begin to unfold at the store, drawing them closer and reigniting their past feelings.

As the two navigate their complex relationship, a tempting offer from a big entertainment company to buy Rewind Rentals forces Amelia to decide between preserving her family's legacy or taking a leap into an uncertain future. Amidst the challenges of saving the store and confronting their past, Amelia and Flynn must decide if they can trust each other again and if love is worth the risk.

Also by Jax Wilder

Coral Cove Series

Sleighed by Love

Harvesting Love

Dawning Desire

Knead You Now

Love Rewound

Haunted by Her

Perfect Lover Spell

Tarot Fantasies Series

The Devil's Temptations

Strength of the Beast

Hanged Passions

6 of Cups

Death's Embrace

Jax Wilder

Additional Books by

Rainbow Quartz Publishing

Lorelai Hamilton

Find Your Bliss

Teenage Witch's Grimoire

Tarot Reflection Journal

Tarot Refection Journal Coloring The Tarot

The Eclectic Witch's Grimoire

Dream Journal

Teenage Tarot

Tarot Tales and Magic Spells

Arcane In Verse

Miranda Levi

From A Youth A Fountain Did Flow

The Sea Withdrew

A Tear In Time

Mo(ther) Na(ture)

In Orion's Hands

Jackson Anhalt

From The 911 Files

Lorelai Hamilton

Find Your Bliss

Teenage Witch's Grimoire

Tarot Reflection Journal

Tarot Refection Journal Coloring The Tarot

The Eclectic Witch's Grimoire

Dream Journal

Teenage Tarot

Tarot Tales and Magic Spells

Arcane In Verse

Isla Watts

A Fairy Bad Day

Surprise! You're a Vampire

Gorgeous, Gorgeous, Gorgons

Mork The Handsome Orc

Adopted By Werewolves

Bite Me If You Can

That's The Spirit!

Rose Dawson's Book Journals

My Time With The Fairies

Enchanted Escapades

Enchanted Escapades

Dewey Decimal Diaries

Siren's Songbook

Pride and Prejudice

Bibliophile's Bounty

Book of Books Journal

Pages & Passages Reading Journal

Bookworm's Companion Reading Journal & Tracker

About the Author

Jax Wilder is a passionate romance author hailing from a charming small town nestled in the picturesque Pacific Northwest. With a heart full of love and an unyielding belief in the power of happily ever afters, Jax weaves enchanting tales of love and connection that leave readers captivated.

Jax's novels are a reflection of her commitment to celebrating the magic of love, and her characters' journeys mirror the warmth and happiness she has found in her own life. Join her on the enchanting journey of love, passion, and enduring connection through her heartfelt romance novels.

Jax Wilder

www.ingramcontent.com/pod-product-compliance
Lightning Source LLC
Chambersburg PA
CBHW030520130626
46549CB00007B/3070